Crocodiles and Alligators

Therese Shea

PowerKiDS press™

New York

Published in 2007 by The Rosen Publishing Group, Inc.
29 East 21st Street, New York, NY 10010

Book Design: Daniel Hosek

Photo Credits: Cover © Brian Upton/Shutterstock; p. 5 © Emin Kuliyev/Shutterstock; p. 7 (crocodile)
© Henry William Fu/Shutterstock; p. 7 (snake, turtle) © Bruce MacQueen/Shutterstock; p. 7 (alligator)
© Lisa James/Shutterstock; p. 7 (lizard) © Bruce Amos/Shutterstock; p. 9 © Stefan Ekernas/Shutterstock
p. 11 (crocodile) © John Austin/Shutterstock; p. 11 (alligator) © Jeff Carpenter/Shutterstock; p. 13 ©
Fred Murray/Shutterstock; p. 15 © Christian McCarty/Shutterstock; p. 17 © Nicholas Rjabow/
Shutterstock; p. 19 © Torsten Blackwood/AFP/Getty Images; p. 21 © Robert King/Getty Images;
p. 22 © Krige van Rensburg/Shutterstock.

Library of Congress Cataloging-in-Publication Data

Shea, Therese.
  Crocodiles and alligators / Therese Shea.
    p. cm. - (Big bad biters)
  Includes bibliographical references and index.
  ISBN-13: 978-1-4042-3523-X
  ISBN-10: 1-4042-3523-X
  1. Crocodiles—Juvenile literature. 2. Alligators—Juvenile literature. I. Title. II. Series: Shea, Therese. Big
bad biters.
  QL666.C925S54 2007
  597.98'2-dc22
                                2006014526

Manufactured in the United States of America

Contents

A Log with Eyes!

Imagine you are sitting by a pond. You see a log moving in the water. The log has eyes! That's not a log! It's a crocodile! O is it an alligator?

Both crocodiles and alligators are animals that live in or near water. They have bumpy skin and long tails. Their strong jaws have many sharp teeth. They may look scary, but their appearance helps them in their surroundings. Let's learn more about these big bad biters!

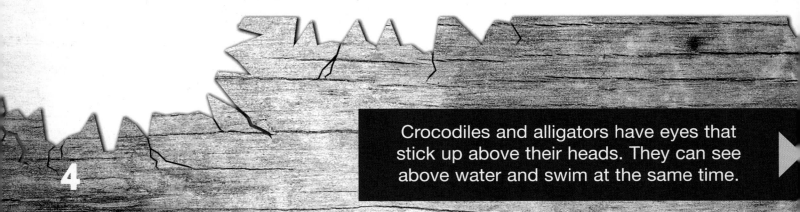

Crocodiles and alligators have eyes that stick up above their heads. They can see above water and swim at the same time.

What Is a Reptile?

Crocodiles and alligators are **reptiles**. A reptile is an animal with dry, scaly skin. It has a **backbone** and breathes air. All reptiles are cold-blooded. This means their surroundings control their body **temperature**. When a crocodile or alligator gets too cold, it lies in the sun to warm up. When it gets too warm, it lies in the shade or dives into water to cool down.

Alligators usually live in cooler places than crocodiles. Alligators may also **hibernate** in mud holes in the winter.

Alligators, crocodiles, snakes, lizards, and turtles are all reptiles.

crocodile

snake

alligator

lizard

turtle

7

Croc and Gator Bodies

Crocodiles and alligators have long bodies with short legs. Alligators may grow to be 12 feet (3.7 m) long or more. Some crocodiles are over 20 feet (6.1 m) long! Crocodiles and alligators have long, thick tails. They swim by moving their tails from side to side.

Crocodiles are a dull gray-green color. Alligator skin looks greener. They both have rough skin with bumps made from tiny bones on their backs. The skin on their bellies is smooth.

Crocodiles and alligators may keep growing their whole lives. Bones from crocodiles that lived long ago tell us some were up to 50 feet (15.2 m) long!

9

Open Wide!

Crocodiles and alligators have powerful **muscles** in their jaws that help them bite down hard. However, they have weak muscles to open their jaws.

To tell the difference between a crocodile and an alligator, look at their mouths. Most crocodiles have pointed **snouts**, while alligators have rounded snouts. The fourth tooth of the lower jaw is extra long in both animals. However, this tooth sticks up over the upper jaw in a crocodile's closed mouth.

Can you see the differences between this crocodile and this alligator?

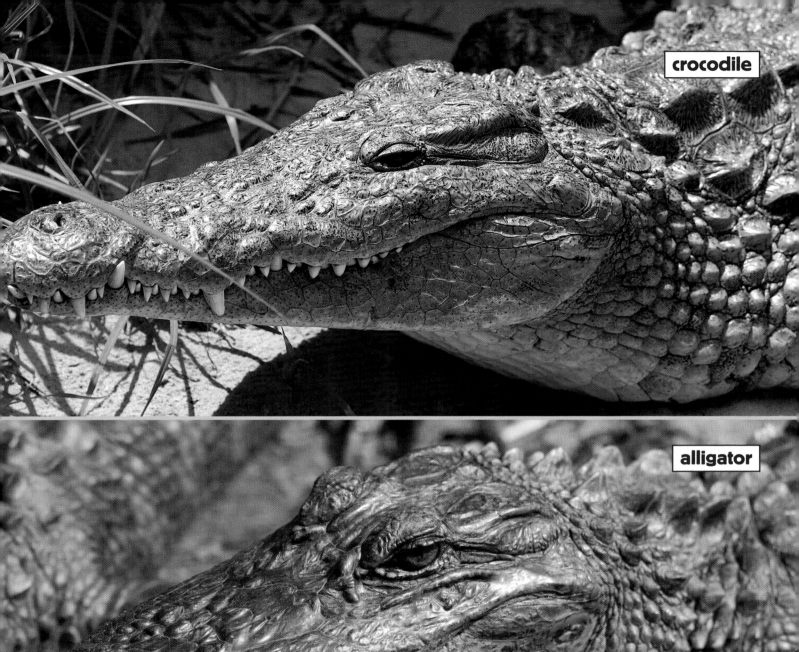

crocodile

alligator

11

Where Do They Live?

Most crocodiles live in warm parts of Africa, Australia, and Southeast Asia. Some live in southern Florida, Mexico, Central America, and South America. Crocodiles are mostly found in saltwater areas. Their special tongues help them get rid of the extra salt that gets into their bodies.

Alligators live in the southeastern United States and eastern China. They have a special tongue for salt water, too. However, it doesn't work as well as a crocodile's tongue. Alligators are mostly found in freshwater.

Crocodiles and alligators live in slow-moving rivers and large bodies of water that aren't very deep.

13

What Do They Eat?

Alligators and crocodiles mostly eat small animals that live in or near water, such as fish, birds, frogs, and turtles. They swallow them whole. Sometimes they eat larger animals, including deer, dogs, buffalo, monkeys, and cattle.

Crocodiles and alligators can grab a large animal's body part with their strong jaws. Then they twist in the water until the part comes off. They throw the body part in the air until it falls down their throat. Scary!

Crocodiles and alligators may attack people. It is always a good idea to leave them alone.

15

Babies

Crocodiles and alligators lay eggs. They make nests out of grass and plants. Some crocodiles bury their eggs in the sand. Most mothers stay and protect the nest. When the baby crocodiles and alligators are about to **hatch**, they make sounds inside their eggs. Their mothers hear these sounds and dig the eggs out of the nest. After the babies hatch, their mothers sometimes carry them to the water in their mouths. Mothers look after their babies for about a year.

Baby crocodiles and alligators have a tough extra bit of skin on their snouts to help them break out of their eggs. This "egg tooth" later becomes part of their skin.

A Part of Nature

Crocodiles and alligators look scary and can hurt people. So why do we need these large reptiles? Crocodiles and alligators are an important part of nature. They eat fish, snakes turtles, birds, and other animals. Without crocodiles and alligators, too many of these animals might exist. They might eat too much and cause other animals to die. Crocodiles and alligators help keep their surroundings healthy.

These alligators are very hungry after hibernating all winter. They are jumping in the air to catch a piece of meat.

19

Hunted!

Nothing hunts alligators and crocodiles—except people! People use alligator and crocodile skin for leather to make shoes, bags, and other kinds of clothing. Some people even ea their meat! Alligators and crocodiles were once hunted so mucl that some kinds became **endangered**.

Laws were set up to stop hunters. The alligator population has grown again. However, some kinds of crocodiles are still in danger of dying out.

These alligator heads are being sold as decorations. Large heads may cost $500 each.

21

Cool Croc and Gator Facts

Here are some more cool facts about crocodiles and alligators:

- They can hold their breath underwater for more than an hour.
- They can swim up to 20 miles (32 km) per hour.
- They can run on land up to 11 miles (18 km) per hour.
- They store fat in their tails so they don't have to eat for a long time.

These big bad biters are really amazing. Just keep your distance!

Glossary

ackbone (BAK-bohn) The main bones along the middle of the back of many animals. The backbone is made up of many smaller bones.

ndangered (in-DAYN-jurd) In danger of no longer existing.

atch (HACH) To break out of an egg.

ibernate (HY-buhr-nayt) To sleep through the winter.

uscle (MUH-suhl) A part of a body that is connected to bones and helps them move.

eptile (REHP-tyl) An animal that is usually covered with scales, such as an alligator or a lizard. A reptile is as warm or as cold as the air around it.

out (SNOUT) A long nose that sticks out.

mperature (TEHM-puhr-chur) How hot or cold something is.

Index

Web Sites

Due to the changing nature of Internet links, PowerKids Press has developed an online list of Web sites related to the subject of this book. This site is updated regularly. Please use this link to access the list:
http://www.powerkidslinks.com/biters/crocalli/